A NOTE TO PARENTS

Reading Aloud with Your Child

Research shows that reading books aloud is the single most valuable support parents can provide in helping children learn to read.

- Be a ham! The more enthusiasm you display, the more your child will enjoy the book.
- Run your finger underneath the words as you read to signal that the print carries the story.
- Leave time for examining the illustrations more closely; encourage your child to find things in the pictures.
- Invite your youngster to join in whenever there's a repeated phrase in the text.
- Link up events in the book with similar events in your child's life.
- If your child asks a question, stop and answer it. The book can be a means to learning more about your child's thoughts.

Listening to Your Child Read Aloud

The support of your attention and praise is absolutely crucial to your child's continuing efforts to learn to read.

- If your child is learning to read and asks for a word, give it immediately so that the meaning of the story is not interrupted. DO NOT ask your child to sound out the word.
- On the other hand, if your child initiates the act of sounding out, don't intervene.
- If your child is reading along and makes what is called a miscue, listen for the sense of the miscue. If the word "road" is substituted for the word "street," for instance, no meaning is lost. Don't stop the reading for a correction.
- If the miscue makes no sense (for example, "horse" for "house"), ask your child to reread the sentence because you're not sure you understand what's just been read.
- Above all else, enjoy your child's growing command of print and make sure you give lots of praise. *You are your child's first teacher — and the most important one. Praise from you is critical for further risk-taking and learning.*

— Priscilla Lynch
Ph.D., New York University
Educational Consultant

To my favorite creatures, Genevieve and Gwen
—J.B.S.

Text copyright © 1997 by Judith Bauer Stamper.
Illustrations copyright © 1997 by Tim Raglin.
All rights reserved. Published by Scholastic Inc.
HELLO READER!, CARTWHEEL BOOKS, and the
CARTWHEEL BOOKS logo are registered trademarks of Scholastic Inc.

Library of Congress Cataloging-in-Publication Data

Stamper, Judith Bauer.
    Five creepy creatures / by Judith Bauer Stamper ; illustrated by Tim Raglin.
      p.   cm. — (Hello reader! Level 4)
    "Cartwheel books."
    Contents: Stop that coffin! — Who's there? — The new neighbor — In old trees — The strange visitor.
    Summary: A collection of five easy-to-read stories about creepy creatures.
    ISBN 0-590-92154-1 (alk. paper)
    1. Horror tales, American. 2. Children's stories, American. [1. Horror stories. 2. Short stories.] I. Raglin, Tim, ill. II. Title. III. Series.
PZ7.S78612Fg   1997
[E] — dc20
96-31836
CIP
AC

12 11 10 9 8 7 6 5 4 3 2 1   7 8 9/9 0 1 2/0

Printed in the U.S.A.   24

First Scholastic printing, October 1997

by Judith Bauer Stamper
Illustrated by Tim Raglin

Hello Reader! — Level 4

SCHOLASTIC INC. Cartwheel B·O·O·K·S ®
New York Toronto London Auckland Sydney

STOP THAT COFFIN!

One night, a boy took a walk
in a graveyard.
His little sister came along.
They walked along a path
lit by a big, yellow moon.
The boy was feeling scared.
But he acted cool and calm.

"I'm not afraid of graveyards,"
his sister said.
"You aren't?" the boy asked.
"Not a bit," his sister answered
with a smile.

They walked on past
the white tombstones.
Then they saw a big hole
dug in the ground.
"Dare you to look in that hole,"
his sister said.
"I'm not scared," the boy said
in a shaky voice.
"Then look in it," his sister dared.

The boy walked over to the hole.
His knees were shaking.
He inched up to the edge of the hole.
Then he looked in.

And a big, brown coffin
jumped out of the hole!
It started to chase the boy
and his sister.

They took off running.
But the coffin followed
right behind them!

BUMP! BUMP! BUMP!
The coffin bumped and jumped
along the cemetery path.
"We've got to get out of here!"
the boy screamed.
"I'm not afraid of that coffin,"
his sister said and laughed.

They ran until they reached the gates
of the graveyard.
They ran out onto the sidewalk.
"I think we lost it!" the boy said.

BUMP! BUMP! BUMP!
The coffin bumped and jumped
onto the sidewalk behind them.
"Run!" the boy screamed.
The coffin was so close
it was breathing down their necks!

The boy and his sister ran
until they reached their house.
They ran up the five front steps.
The coffin was right behind them.
BUMP! BUMP! BUMP!
That coffin jumped right up
those five steps.

The boy tried and tried to open
the front door.
But it was locked.
And there was the coffin!

His sister turned around
to stare at the coffin.
She reached in her pocket
and pulled out a box.
Then she took a cough drop out
and handed it to the coffin.
"This will stop that coffin!"
she said to her brother.

And the coffin stopped and went away.

WHO'S THERE?

KNOCK, KNOCK.
Who's there?
Weirdo.
Weirdo who?
Weirdo you think you're going?

KNOCK, KNOCK.
Who's there?
Horror.
Horror who?
Horror ya doing?

KNOCK, KNOCK.

Who's there?

Werewolf.

Werewolf who?

Werewolf I find a bathroom?

KNOCK, KNOCK.

Who's there?

Voodoo.

Voodoo who?

Voodoo you think you are?

KNOCK, KNOCK.

Who's there?

Boo.

Boo who?

Don't cry. I'm not going to eat you!

THE NEW NEIGHBOR

One hot, sleepy, summer day,
a new neighbor moved in.
Howard watched from his window.
The movers carried in a big, green chair.
Then they carried in a huge bed.
All day long, they carried in one thing
after another.

Howard watched and waited.
He wanted to see his new neighbor.
Finally, at midnight, a big, black car
pulled up to the house.
A dark figure got out and went into
the house.

Howard fell asleep.
He dreamed a long, weird dream
about the new neighbor.
He remembered it all the next morning.

"My new neighbor is a monster,"
he told his best friend.
"Don't tell anybody else."

Right away, the best friend told
another friend.

"Howard's new neighbor is a monster.
Don't tell anybody else."

That friend told her little brother.
"Howard's new neighbor is a monster.
Don't tell anybody else."

Soon, everyone in town knew
that Howard's new neighbor
was a monster.
No one wanted to go near the house.
Paperboys refused to deliver there.
Even the mailman ran to and from
the house.

Howard began to feel guilty.
He hadn't really seen his neighbor yet.
He had just *dreamed* he was a monster.
And now everyone was scared of him.
Howard knew it was wrong
to start a rumor.
He decided to apologize
to his new neighbor.

That night, he went to his neighbor's
house.
He knocked on the door.

No one came.

Howard started to get a little nervous.

But he had made up his mind.

He knocked on the door again.

Finally, he heard footsteps
coming toward the door.

But no one opened the door.

Howard called through the door,
"I'm sorry I called you a monster."

Then the door creaked open.

"That's all right,"
the new neighbor said.
"I am one!"

IN OLD TREES

In old trees,
there are holes
where the wood has rotted out.
But don't put your hand in to feel,
because...

In old trees,
there are holes
where the wood has rotted out,
and creatures live there
that no one sees.
But don't put your hand in to feel,
because . . .

In old trees,
there are holes
where the wood has rotted out,
and creatures live there
that no one sees.
They have yellow eyes and long noses
and sharp teeth.
But don't put your hand in to feel,
because ...

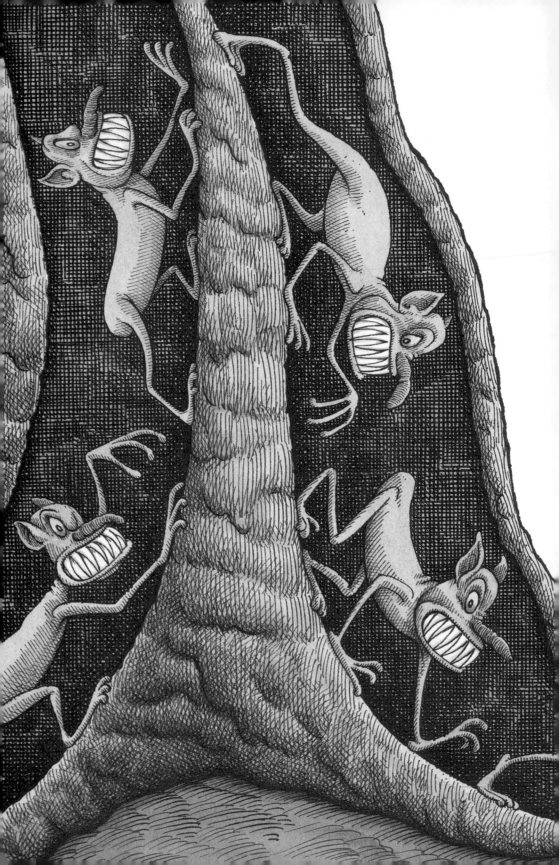

In old trees,
there are holes
where the wood has rotted out,
and creatures live there
that no one sees.
They have yellow eyes and long noses
and sharp teeth,
and they run up and down
and into the ground.
But don't put your hand in to feel,
because...

In old trees,
there are holes
where the wood has rotted out,
and creatures live there
that no one sees.
They have yellow eyes and long noses
and sharp teeth,
and they run up and down
and into the ground.
And if you put your hand in to feel...

THEY'LL TICKLE YOU!

THE STRANGE VISITOR

Once there was a lonely, old woman
who lived in a house in the woods.
Each night, she sat by the fire
spinning her wool.
And so she sat.
And so she spun.
And so she waited
for someone to come.

One night, the door creaked open.
CREAK.
And in came —
a big pair of feet.

The feet stomped over to the fire
right beside the woman.
"How strange," the woman said.
And still she sat.
And still she spun.
And still she waited
for someone to come.

Then the door creaked open again.
CREAK.
And in came a pair of short,
hairy legs.
The legs sat themselves down
on the big feet.
"How strange," the woman said.
And still she sat.
And still she spun.
And still she waited
for someone to come.

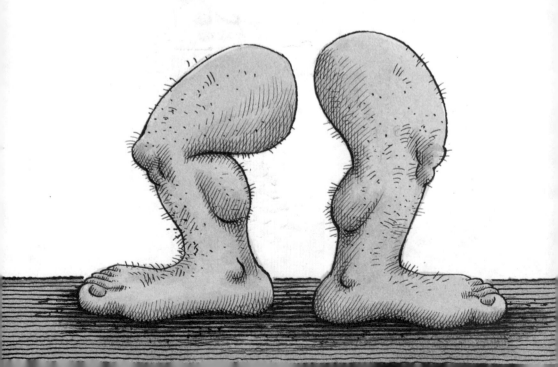

Once again, the door creaked open.
CREAK.
And in came a pair of huge hips.
The hips sat themselves down
on the short, hairy legs.
"How strange," the woman said.
And still she sat.
And still she spun.
And still she waited
for someone to come.

Then the door creaked open again.
CREAK.
And in came a broad chest and shoulders.
The chest and shoulders
sat themselves down on the huge hips.
"How strange," the woman said.
And still she sat.
And still she spun.
And still she waited
for someone to come.

Again, the door creaked open.
CREAK.
And in came a set of long arms
with fat fingers.
The arms and fingers
sat themselves down on the broad chest
and shoulders.
"How strange," the woman said.
And still she sat.
And still she spun.
And still she waited
for someone to come.

The door creaked open one more time.
CREAK.
And in rolled a huge, horrible head.

The head sat itself down
on top of the broad chest and shoulders.
"How strange," said the woman.

Then she asked, "How did you get
such big feet?"
"MUCH STOMPING. MUCH STOMPING,"
the visitor said.
"How did you get such short, hairy legs?"
"MUCH RUNNING. MUCH RUNNING."
"How did you get such huge hips?"
"MUCH EATING. MUCH EATING."
"How did you get such a broad chest
and shoulders?"
"MUCH FIGHTING. MUCH FIGHTING."
"How did you get such long arms
and fat fingers?"
"MUCH GRABBING. MUCH GRABBING."
"How did you get such a huge, horrible head?"
"MUCH THINKING. MUCH THINKING."

"Why did you come here?" the woman asked.
And the visitor replied . . .

"BECAUSE I NEED A HUG!"